Mystery of the Disappearing Dolphin

Mystery
of the
Disappearing
Dolphin

BY JANELLE DILLER

ILLUSTRATIONS BY ADAM TURNER

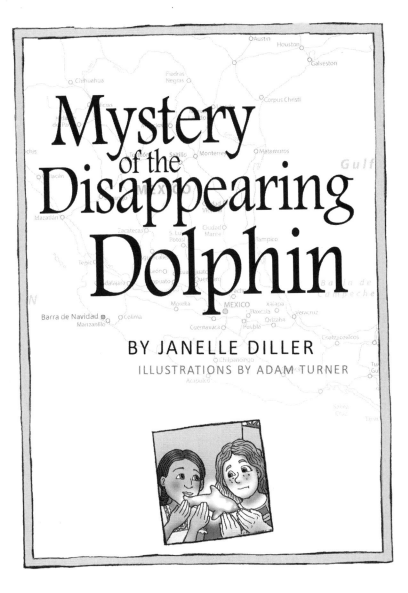

Published by WorldTrek Publishing

Copyright © 2014 by Pack-n-Go Girls

Printed in the USA

Visit our Web site at www.packngogirls.com.

This is a work of fiction. Names, characters, places, and incidents either are the product of the author's imagination or are used fictitiously. The town of Barra de Navidad, Jalisco, is real, and it's a wonderful place to visit. Any other resemblance to actual events, locales, organizations, or persons, living or dead, is entirely coincidental and beyond the intent of either the author or the publisher.

Illustrations by Adam Turner

ISBN 978-1-936376-15-5

Cataloging-in-Publication Data available from the Library of Congress.

Mystery of the Disappearing Dolphin is the second book in the Pack-n-Go Girls Mexico adventures. The first book, *Mystery of the Thief in the Night*, tells how Izzy and Patti first met. Here's a bit about the book:

Izzy's family sails into a quiet lagoon in Mexico and drops their anchor. Izzy can't wait to explore the pretty little village, eat yummy tacos, and practice her Spanish. When she meets nine-year-old Patti, Izzy's thrilled. Now she can do all that and have a new friend to play with too. Life is perfect.

At least it's perfect until they realize there's a midnight thief on the loose!

Contents

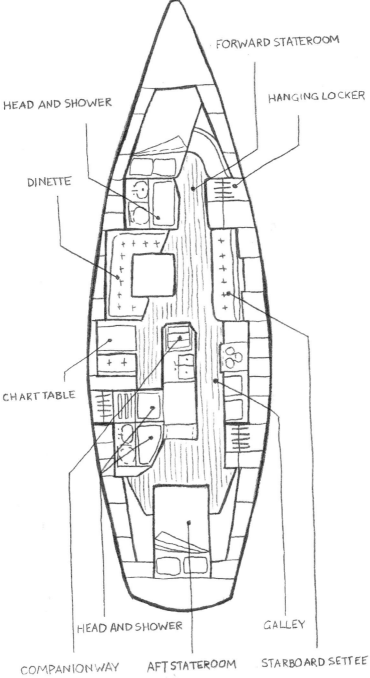

FORWARD STATEROOM

HANGING LOCKER

HEAD AND SHOWER

DINETTE

CHART TABLE

HEAD AND SHOWER

GALLEY

COMPANIONWAY

AFT STATEROOM

STARBOARD SETTEE

Meet the Characters

Izzy Bennett loves sailing on Dream Catcher. Even more? She loves playing with her new friend, Patti.

Patti Delgado is excited that Izzy is ready for their next adventure together in Barra de Navidad.

Mr. Dawson is Izzy's uncle. He loves visiting his niece in Mexico even though traveling makes him really nervous.

Mr. Bennett

is Izzy's dad. It's his dream come true to spend this year sailing with his family.

Mrs. Bennett is Izzy's

mom. She's happy their family can discover the culture of Mexico in such a fun way.

Mrs. Delgado is Patti's

mom. She's thrilled that Patti can learn about the US with her new friend.

The Disappearing Dolphin

can reappear anywhere!

And now, the mystery begins . . .

Mystery of the Disappearing Dolphin

Chapter 1

The Dream

Nothing made sense.

Nothing.

Izzy watched the spooky shadow float into her stateroom. It swam through the air, diving and rising over her bed. With each dip, it crept closer and closer. She tried to scream to scare the shadow away, but no sound came out. She felt frozen in her bed. Her legs and arms wouldn't move.

She yelled again. And again, there was no noise.

Her heart pounded.

The gray shape shifted into something she knew.

A fish. A giant fish. A fish that purred like a cat.

Izzy couldn't figure out how the fish got inside Dream Catcher, the sailboat she lived on. The silver monster drifted over her bed. It dove toward her again. Streaks of blue light flashed over its back.

Slowly, it swished its tail up and down, up and down. And then it twisted and flipped like a dolphin.

The dolphin sang to her in perfect English. "Don't worry. Be happy."

Izzy hadn't known dolphins could speak English or sing. She answered in Spanish. She didn't know what she said, but she knew she'd said it perfectly. Izzy loved that she knew more Spanish than the dolphin.

The dolphin chattered at her. Clang, clang, clang. It sounded like a metal baseball bat hitting the school's jungle gym. Kind of.

Clang, clang. Clang. Clang, clang.

Izzy opened her eyes.

The Dream

Poof! The dolphin disappeared.

Izzy shook her head to clear it. Katie Kitty still slept in her favorite spot. The cat lay between Izzy and the hull, or outside wall, of the boat.

What a weird dream.

Her heart still pounded. The dream seemed spooky real. She half expected the dolphin to float back into her stateroom.

Izzy heard the clanging again. Now she knew the sound. The wind must have picked up. The lines that raised the sails banged against the mast, the tall pole that held the main sail. Izzy tried to think of the word her dad used.

Halyards. That was it. That was the sailing word for them. The halyards clanged against the mast.

The wind rarely blew in the morning. A storm must be coming in. That never happened this time of year.

Weird dream.

Weird weather.

A weird start to the day.

Izzy crawled out of bed and pulled the sheets off. Her mom would put fresh ones on later because her Uncle Rob and Aunt Ella were arriving today. They would sleep in her stateroom, or bedroom. Everything on a boat had a different name than the same thing in a house. It was like talking another language.

Izzy would sleep in the living room, or salon, of the boat. Izzy hoped her mom would let her sleep in the cockpit instead. Izzy loved sleeping out in the fresh air.

A rooster crowed on shore. Another rooster crowed back.

Izzy never heard roosters crowing in their marina in Seattle. That's where she and her mom and dad lived before they started sailing in Mexico.

She dug around in the cubby below her bed,

or berth. She pulled out clean shorts and a clean tanktop. She wished she hadn't put her sailboat T-shirt in the laundry. She should have thought ahead so she could wear her favorite shirt when her favorite aunt came to Dream Catcher.

She ran her fingers through her red curls. A brush would be better. This was easier.

Izzy thought about the dream again. It had been so easy to talk Spanish in the dream. Why couldn't it be like that in real life?

She headed out to the galley, or kitchen. Izzy's mom and dad sat in the cockpit, a few feet up and outside. She could hear them whispering. They didn't do that often. They only did it when they were mad about something. They had a hard time keeping a fight secret in a small space like a boat. She hated when they fought.

Her mom had left a new box of milk on the counter for her cereal. When they first started sailing in Mexico, Izzy thought milk in a box was too strange. Milk should always stay in the refrigerator. Her mom thought it was too cool, though. They could keep milk in a cabinet till they needed it. That was great because they didn't have much refrigerator space on the boat. Her mom said a lot of Mexican homes didn't have refrigerators. Milk in a box made it easier for them to have milk more often.

Izzy poured granola into a bowl. She cut up a few fresh strawberries and added some milk. Then she sat down at the table and opened up her math book.

"Morning, sweetheart," her mom called down to her from the cockpit.

"Morning, Izzy Lizzie," her dad said.

"Morning," Izzy said back. She took a bite of crunchy cereal.

Izzy stared at her multiplication problems.

The Dream

The weird dream filled her head. The wind rattled the halyards again.

Something just felt spooky with it all. No. It felt creepy. The talking dolphin seemed so real.

She tried to focus on her math.

"I'm telling you, Annie," Mr. Bennett whispered. For a whisper, it was a loud one. "The first thing Rob will say is that it's too hot. Then he'll complain about the taxi driver. Then he'll grumble about how we live on a boat."

Izzy's mom sighed.

Her dad kept right on talking. "I don't even know why he's coming to Mexico. He hates traveling and gripes about anything that's not like home. Remember when they went to Germany last year? Whine, whine, whine. Every single email."

Izzy wished they'd stop fighting. Even more? She wished they would just let her go to Hotel Siesta and play with her new friend, Patti. But then she also had to wish Patti would be out of school early.

She sighed and stared at her multiplication problems again.

Her dad couldn't stop talking. "Rob even gets nervous about going to California." He snorted in disbelief. "I mean, for goodness sakes, California!"

Izzy looked up toward the cockpit. She could see her dad's long legs. His tanned hands were spread out on his knees. He leaned in towards Izzy's mom.

Mrs. Bennett said something. Izzy couldn't hear

what she said.

"I know Ella is your sister. And I know if your sister comes to visit she's going to bring her husband," Mr. Bennett muttered. "All I'm saying is that he complains too much. And he's suspicious about anyone who isn't just like him. So that means he's suspicious about the entire rest of the world."

Suspicious. Izzy rolled that word around in her mouth. She wasn't sure what it meant, but it didn't sound nice. She wrote it down like it sounded: suss-pish-us. She'd ask her dad what the word meant when he was in a better mood.

"I just don't like having him stay on the boat," her dad whispered. Once more, it wasn't much of a whisper.

Mrs. Bennett murmured something back.

Mr. Bennett snorted and said, "That tightwad? Rob would never pay for a room if he can stay for free. And we can't afford to pay for a hotel room for them." By now, he'd completely forgotten he was supposed to be quiet. "Unless you want to quit sailing earlier and go back to Seattle."

There it was. Money again. They always had to watch their budget.

It meant Izzy always had something to worry about. As if she didn't have enough already because she lived on a boat. What did the dolphin say? "Don't worry. Be happy." She could do the happy part of that. But stop worrying? Not a chance.

"Let's see," Izzy said out loud. "Twenty-seven times thirty-four." Maybe her mom and dad had forgotten she could hear them. "Seven times four is twenty-eight. Carry the two—" She tapped her pencil on the paper.

"Sorry, Izzy Lizzie," Mr. Bennett called down to her. "We'll try not to talk so loud."

"You could just let me go kayaking. Then you wouldn't have to whisper," Izzy said. It was worth a try.

Her mom laughed. Izzy liked the sound. It meant maybe her mom and dad weren't super mad at each other.

Mr. Bennett leaned over to look at Izzy. "I think we'd all like to go kayaking for a week while Uncle Rob is on the boat."

"Mark!" Mrs. Bennett said. She laughed again though. She glanced at her watch. "Speaking of, we should head to shore to meet them at Hotel Siesta. Rob and Ella's cab should be here soon."

Mr. Bennett groaned.

Izzy said a silent cheer. At least she wouldn't have to do schoolwork today. She put away her math book. She gathered up her hat, flip-flops, and sunglasses. Then she put on sunscreen. She already had plenty of freckles, thank you very much. At the last minute, she stuffed her swimsuit in her bag in case her mom let her swim at the hotel with Patti.

They all climbed into Ringee Dingee, their trusty little boat that would take them to shore. In just the last few weeks, Izzy had become extra glad for it. She patted the sides of the rubber boat.

When the family had first arrived in the Barra de Navidad lagoon, they worried a thief would steal their small boat. Izzy loved knowing her friend Patti and she were kind of local heroes. They had figured out who was stealing the dinghies in the lagoon. Now all the boaters felt safe to anchor again in the calm, protected water.

The three of them zipped to shore. They pulled up to the dinghy dock at the Hotel Siesta and tied the boat to a cleat.

"There you are!" a man's voice boomed. "Finally."

Izzy caught her dad rolling his eyes at her mom.

Her mom raised her eyebrow at her dad.

Rob and Ella Dawson waved at them from a table in the restaurant that was part of Hotel Siesta.

The Dream

Izzy ran over and threw her arms around her favorite aunt.

"Well, Izzy, aren't you darling in your straw hat and pink sunglasses?" Mrs. Dawson said. "You just get prettier every time we see you."

"Still the smartest kid in the class?" Mr. Dawson asked. He gave Izzy a quick, awkward hug.

"Yup. The smartest and the dumbest kid since I'm the ONLY kid in the class right now."

Mr. Dawson laughed at her joke. Izzy knew he would. She knew her uncle could be cranky sometimes, but never with her. Izzy always thought of him as a big, teddy bear kind of guy.

Mrs. Bennett hugged Mr. Dawson. He gave her a quick peck on the cheek and shook Mr. Bennett's hand. "Good to see you, Mark and Annie," he said. He took off his baseball cap and fanned his face. "Boy, I don't know how you can take this heat. It's too much for me."

Mr. and Mrs. Bennett looked at each other.

"And that taxi driver? He was a crazy man. Drove 100 miles an hour down part of the highway. How nuts is that?"

"Uh, Uncle Rob," Izzy said. "They use kilometers here instead of miles. I think that was 100 kilometers an hour." Izzy did the math in her head. "So he was driving 60 miles an hour."

"Huh?" Mr. Dawson wrinkled up his nose.

The Dream

"Oh, well it was still too fast. He was crazy. Just crazy." He sat back down in his chair. "I'm starving. Let's grab some lunch before we get on that dinky sailboat of yours. Honestly, I don't know why you're living on a boat. All crammed together like that." He shook his head and picked up the menu.

Mrs. Dawson's shoulders drooped a bit.

Mr. and Mrs. Bennett looked at each other again.

Izzy sighed. It was going to be a long, long week.

Chapter 2

Tianguis Day!

"¡Hola, Izzy! Hola Señor y Señora Bennett." Izzy's
friend Patti waved at them from across the room.
She stepped back into the kitchen and called out to
the Bennetts, *"Sólo un momento."*

Just one minute.

Izzy loved that she was learning more Spanish
every time she hung out with Patti. It was going to
be way cool to go back to school in Seattle and be
able to speak another language.

Tianguis Day

Patti arrived at the table to take their orders. *"Buenas tardes. ¿Como estan ustedes?"* Good afternoon. How are you?

Izzy answered for the family. *"Bien, gracias."* Fine thanks. *"Patti, este es el Señor y la Señora Dawson. Son mis tios de Seattle. Van a pasar una semana con nosotros en el velero."*

She turned to her aunt and uncle and told them what she'd said. "Uncle Rob and Aunt Ella, I just said that you're my uncle and aunt from Seattle and you're spending a week with us on our sailboat. This is my new friend, Patti. Her mom and dad own the hotel and restaurant. We've had a lot of fun playing together."

Mr. Dawson's eyebrows scrunched together and his eyes narrowed. He looked unhappy for some reason. Izzy hoped Patti didn't notice.

"Bienvenidos a Hotel Siesta Café," Patti said and gave them a wide smile. "Welcome to Hotel Siesta Café. It's a pleasure to meet you."

"Ellos están felices de conocerte, también." They're happy to meet you, too. Izzy knew that was true for her aunt for sure.

"My goodness," Mrs. Dawson said. "You sound just like a native, Izzy. Are we going to be able to speak Spanish that well by the time we leave?"

"Por supuesto," Patti said. "Of course. But you won't learn unless you try. Right, Izzy?"

Mr. Dawson frowned. "Where did you learn to speak English so well?"

Izzy glanced at her dad who frowned too. Her uncle had asked a good question. Izzy just couldn't figure out why he sounded a little mad.

"Patti practices with the tourists who come to their restaurant and hotel," Izzy said quickly. "Like me. And she's helping me learn Spanish, too. She's a good teacher."

"Well, it sounds like you're both doing a great job," Mrs. Dawson said. "I always wanted to learn another language."

"It's never too late," Mrs. Bennett said.

"Well, it is for me," Mr. Dawson said. "I only want to speak English." He turned to Patti. "Young lady, what's good on the menu?"

"Everything. But the *enchiladas de Patti* are especially good today. They have chicken and cheese and *salsa verde*. That's a green salsa." She smiled happily. "I helped my mom make up the recipe, so she named them after me."

"I'm sure they're delicious. I'd love to try that," Mrs. Dawson said. She handed Patti her menu.

"I'm sticking with a hamburger and french fries," Mr. Dawson said. "Make sure the meat is fried

19

good." He leaned over and whispered to Izzy, "Best advice I can give you, kiddo? Don't ever drink the water in another country, and get your meat well done. You don't want to pick up any bugs." He shook his head. "Worst thing ever is to get sick when you're away from home."

Izzy watched to see if her dad would roll his eyes. He didn't, but he looked like he wanted to.

Her aunt sighed. "Rob, *no one* wants to get sick when they're away from home. But you worry too much. You need to just go with the flow and have fun. I'll bet Izzy is just fine when she travels."

Izzy smiled since she could think of a thousand things she worried about whether she was traveling or at home. "We haven't gotten sick once on our trip."

"You just have to be smart about where and what you eat," Mrs. Bennett said. "We don't eat from every food truck in Seattle, either."

The Bennetts ordered *enchiladas de Patti,* too, and freshly squeezed orange juice. Patti disappeared into the kitchen. A few minutes later she returned with the drinks.

"Izzy, today is *tianguis* day in *el jardín.* You know, the plaza. Do you want to go with me?" Patti asked.

Izzy looked at her mom for permission. Her mom smiled and nodded. "Sure. I'll loan you some money till we get back to the boat."

"Tianguis day?" Mrs. Dawson asked when Patti left.

"It's the market day," Mrs. Bennett said. "All the vendors come to Barra de Navidad. They set up stands, or *puestos,* in the plaza. Here they call the plaza *el jardín.* The garden. They have pottery, clothes, leather goods, jewelry. All kinds of stuff. It's quite fun."

"Perfect, Annie. You know me. I'm always up for a little shopping," Mrs. Dawson said. She turned to her husband. "You guys can go back to the boat and get settled. We'll do a girls afternoon out."

Mr. Dawson huffed. "Are you kidding me, Ella? We didn't come all the way to Mexico just to let you get mugged in some foreign market."

"Great! I guess that means you're coming along," Mrs. Dawson said. "It's a good thing you offered to come." She winked at Izzy. "I was going to need his wallet anyway."

Izzy glanced at her uncle, and her heart beat a little faster. It never occurred to Izzy that they could get mugged in the market.

Chapter 3

The Magic Dolphin

"So is the market dangerous, Patti?"

"Huh?"

Izzy glanced back at her mom and aunt. They were only a few feet behind the girls. But they were so busy catching up they weren't paying any attention to Izzy and Patti. Izzy's uncle walked a few feet behind all of them. He kept glancing in all directions like he expected trouble.

"Is the market dangerous?" Izzy really needed to know how worried she should be.

"*¿Peligroso?*" Patti asked.

"Yes. Dangerous."

"Only if you have money, I guess." Patti laughed.

"You mean there might be pickpockets or we might get mugged?" Izzy asked. The dolphin in her dream had said not to worry. But surely it would understand if she had to worry about pickpockets.

"Pickpokects? Mugged? I don't know what these words mean," Patti said.

Izzy wished she knew more Spanish words. She couldn't ask her mom right now, either. She thought about her dream again. She knew so much Spanish in the dream. She could talk to the strange dolphin.

"Will we get robbed?" Izzy asked using a different word.

"Oh. *Robado.*" Patti laughed again. "Only if you pay too much for something. But I'll help you bargain."

The Magic Dolphin

Izzy felt a tiny bit better even though she wasn't sure Patti really understood her.

Izzy loved the walk to *el jardín*. Everywhere the shops spilled out onto the sidewalk. They walked around crates of oranges, tomatoes, and pineapples. They brushed past racks of brightly colored dresses and made their way through restaurant tables that filled the space to the street. The girls passed the *tortilleria*, the little shop that churned out stacks of fresh tortillas. Izzy breathed in the scent of warm corn flour and heard the clank, clank, clank of the machine.

Usually, this time of day in the plaza only a few people rested in the shade of the trees. Today loads of people wandered past all the covered stands. Izzy's mom and aunt stopped for a moment at a stand, or *puesto*, with wooden bowls and cutting boards.

"*¡Señoras!*" the stand owner called to them. "Take a look. I have everything you need."

Izzy didn't care about wooden bowls. She

couldn't wait to explore the rest of the market with her friend. She smelled fresh tamales and roasting corn. Across the plaza, she heard the gentle tinkling of wind chimes. They passed a *puesto* with fresh berries piled high. It looked like a stand in Pike Place Market in Seattle. For a moment, Izzy felt like she was at home. Next to that *puesto*, a stand had colorful hard candies and *piñatas* hanging from a rod.

"Oh, *piñatas!*" Patti said. "Last year for my birthday I had a butterfly *piñata*. When we broke it open, it had candy and little dolls and school stuff, like pencils and erasers. I can't wait for my next birthday *piñata.*"

"That's what I'm going to ask for on my next birthday, too," Izzy said. "A *piñata* with cool stuff inside. My friends in Seattle would never think to have a *piñata*. We only have birthday cakes and pointy hats and noisy things you blow."

"We have those too," Patti said. "It's fun that

birthdays are a lot the same in the US and in Mexico."

Izzy smelled the next *puesto* before she saw it. "Yum! What's that?"

"*Molé,*" Patti said. "It's made of all kinds of spices and even chocolate." She leaned over and sniffed the reddish brown sauce.

A wrinkled old woman hopped up off her chair. "You want to try?" she asked the girls. She wiped her hands on her apron.

"*Por supuesto,*" Patti said. Of course.

The woman dipped a spoon in the sauce and handed it to Patti. Patti put a dab on her wrist.

"Patti, you shouldn't eat—" Izzy said, but it was too late.

"Mmmmm," Patti said. She licked her lips. "*¡Delicioso!*" She smiled and handed the spoon back to the old woman.

The woman laughed and dipped the spoon in the sauce again. She handed it to Izzy.

Izzy's eyes grew big. She shook her head. How many germs did that spoon have?

Patti poked her and whispered. "It's rude if you turn it down."

Izzy shook her head again. "My mom would kill me if she knew I ate something a stranger offered me."

"Really?" Patti tilted her head. "My mom would be annoyed if I didn't take it. She would say I'm not polite."

"Well, I guess that's one way Americans and Mexicans are the opposite," Izzy said. Then she wondered if she seemed like Uncle Rob to Patti.

"It's okay," Patti said and patted Izzy's arm. She rattled off something in Spanish to the old lady. It made the lady smile and nod her head. "I explained it to her. I told her you're an American and so we're different about some things."

The girls drifted on to a stand with finely

woven straw hats. Izzy glanced back at her mom and aunt. Her uncle stood halfway between the wooden bowl stand and the *molé* stand. It seemed he didn't know whether to stay with his wife or follow the girls. Finally, his feet came unstuck. He headed to where Patti and Izzy were trying on hats. But he kept looking back at his wife and Izzy's mom.

Izzy figured he'd have a sore neck by the end of the shopping time. She wished he didn't feel nervous about being in a place where things were different.

"¡Patti, Patti!" A little boy, maybe three or four years old, poked his head out from under a table. His mop of black hair nearly matched his coffee colored eyes. The boy's grin spread across his face.

"¡Hola, Pancho!" Patti rattled off a bunch of Spanish Izzy didn't understand. Patti bent over and held her arms out. The little boy flew to her. She hugged him and kissed the top of his head.

The Magic Dolphin

"Izzy, this is Pancho. He's the cousin of Luli, one of my friends at school. Isn't he cute? Sometimes Luli brings Pancho when she comes to the hotel, and we go swimming."

Patti turned to the little boy and talked fast again. She moved her hands up and down like a dolphin jumping through the water. It made Pancho laugh, a happy, bubbly sound.

What a sweet little boy, Izzy thought. She bent down and got eye level with him. *"Hola, Pancho. ¿Como estas?"* Hi, Pancho. How are you?

Pancho cautiously reached towards Izzy's red hair. He looked at Patti. Patti looked at Izzy. Izzy nodded her head. *"Esta bien. Puedes tocar mi pelo."* It's okay. You can touch my hair.

"It's pretty. Mexicans don't have red hair. Or curly hair," Patti said. "It's one of the first things I liked about you when I met you."

"Really?" Izzy ran her fingers through her curls.

"That's crazy. I wish my hair would be long and straight like yours. And black. You have beautiful hair."

Patti laughed. "Every Mexican girl has straight black hair. It's not very special."

Pancho pulled Izzy over to a table full of delicate glass animals. The table sparkled in the morning sun. She set her bag down on the ground.

She could spend all day in this place.

The Magic Dolphin

A fish the size of her hand caught her eye.

Only it wasn't a fish. It was a dolphin.

Izzy picked it up.

The dolphin looked clear. As she turned it in the sun, though, blue lines appeared along the fins and over the nose.

Just like the dolphin in her dream.

A shiver ran down her back.

Izzy quickly set the glass creature down. She looked around the market. All around her people shopped and visited. Nothing seemed strange about the day for them.

She couldn't help herself. She picked up the dolphin again. She tilted it back and forth. The light flashed with the motion. "Look, Patti. It's beautiful! See how it catches the sun?"

Just like the dream.

Except dreams shouldn't come to life.

"*Hola, Señoritas,*" a man behind the table said.

"Hola, Señor Gómez," Patti said. She rattled off some Spanish then turned to Izzy. "Señor Gómez is Pancho's father."

Pancho wrapped his arms around his dad's leg and laughed. Señor Gómez tousled the boy's hair and nodded at the girls. "You like the dolphin? For you, a special price. Just 200 pesos."

Izzy took in her breath. She held the dolphin in her hands, the dolphin from her dream. She knew it. But she didn't have even close to 200 pesos. That would be over $15.

"That's way too much," Patti whispered to her. "Do you want me to bargain for you?"

Izzy nodded. "Can you get it for less?"

"It shouldn't be more than 150. Maybe 120 pesos. Let me try."

Izzy put the dolphin down. She shook her head. "Don't bother." She sighed. "Mom gave me 70 pesos, and part of that is an advance on my allowance." She picked the glass creature up again and turned it over. She bent down and showed it to Pancho, turning it to catch the sunlight. *"Es hermoso, sí?"* It's beautiful, isn't it?

She turned to Patti. "What's the word for dolphin in Spanish?"

"Delfín."

Izzy turned to Pancho again. *"Es hermoso como un delfín real es bella."* It's beautiful, just like a real dolphin is beautiful. She sighed and ran her fingers over the smooth glass one more time. She stood up and set the dolphin down again on the table.

Too weird. This is what her dream had been about. Surely, she was supposed to have the glass creature.

But Izzy didn't have the money for it. She sighed.

She picked up a dog with brown lines and a kitten with yellow. A flying parrot that had flashes of green caught her eye, too. But none felt as special as the dolphin.

None of them had been in her dream.

The man picked up the dolphin. "You like this?" the man asked. "I think this is the special one for you. Is *magia.*"

"*¿Magia?*" Izzy looked at Patti. "What does that mean?"

Patti shrugged her shoulders. "I'm not sure in English. In Spanish, it means something special. Like when something happens you can't explain."

Just then, a wind blew through the market. Leaves scattered across the ground and made a clattering sound.

Goosebumps prickled Izzy's arms. She remembered her dream and the wind.

"Magic?" she asked.

"*Sí. Magia.*" Señor Gómez nodded his head. He held the dolphin so the sun shone through the glass.

The Magic Dolphin

It sent a scattering of rainbow colors on the other glass animals.

It took Izzy's breath away. She wished she could catch and keep all of the colors.

Magic. Yes, it truly had to be. She had dreamed about this. It made perfect sense.

Izzy saw Pancho's eyes follow the colors. He laughed his bubbly laugh again.

"Is my last one. I make you special deal. Just today. Only 150 pesos."

"It's beautiful. But I don't have enough money. I only have 70 pesos," Izzy said. She showed Señor Gómez her money. She hoped he might change his mind and give it to her for much less than what he was asking.

"*¡Qué lástima!*" he said and shrugged his shoulders. What a pity. He set the dolphin down again. "Perhaps you find something else?" He picked up a small bird. "I give you this for 90 pesos."

It was still more than she had. And pretty as the bird was, it wasn't the dolphin.

It wasn't what she'd dreamed about.

"Maybe your father buys it for you?" Señor Gómez said. He pointed with his chin to someone behind her.

Izzy turned to see if her dad had come to the market after all. Her uncle stood a couple of feet away. His arms were crossed, and his face looked stern.

Izzy smiled at the vendor. "That's my uncle. He isn't here to buy me anything." Just then, she spotted her mom and aunt. Her aunt carried a bulky bag with her new purchase. From the shape of it, Izzy guessed she'd made a deal on some wooden bowls.

Izzy had a tiny hope in her heart that her mom would give her a bit more money. She turned to her mom and took her hand. "I have to show you the most beautiful dolphin I've ever seen. I don't have quite enough money for it. Can I borrow some?"

Mrs. Bennett bent down to Izzy. "I'm sorry, honey," she said quietly. "Remember? We're on a budget. We don't spend more than we have, especially for something that's just pretty to put on a shelf."

"But it's . . . it's magic." Izzy liked the word the man had used. She didn't know what the magic was, but it had to be true. She had dreamed about this dolphin and now she found it. If her mom could just see the colors it made. "I had a dream about a dolphin like this," she whispered. Her mom just had to understand how important this was.

Mrs. Bennett shook her head. "No, sweetheart," she said.

Izzy knew that's what she would say. She sighed. "Come see it at least." She tugged on her mom's hand to come closer to the table.

The dolphin wasn't where Señor Gómez had set it down. Izzy searched the table for it. But she didn't see it anywhere. Had he just sold it to the customers he was talking to right now?

"Con permiso, Señor Gómez," Izzy said. Excuse me, Mr. Gómez. "Where is the dolphin? Did you sell it?"

Señor Gómez looked at the spot on the table where the dolphin had been. He looked at her funny. He scanned the table. His eyes narrowed and his mouth took on a mean look. He said something in Spanish to Patti.

"No, no, no," Patti said fast. She glanced at Izzy.

"What did he say?" Izzy asked.

Patti shook her head. "It's something that's not true."

"What is it, Patti? You can tell me."

Patti sighed. She glanced at the angry man, then back at Izzy. "He said you must have stolen the dolphin when he wasn't looking."

"What?" Izzy shook her head. "Why would he say that? I'd never steal anything. You believe me, don't you Patti?"

Patti paused. She looked at Señor Gómez, who was shaking his finger at the girls. "Of course I believe you, Izzy." But something in Patti's voice worried Izzy.

"How dare you accuse this girl of stealing!" Mr. Dawson snapped. He pounded his fist on an empty spot on the table. The table rattled and swayed. The glass animals, birds, and fish clinked against each other as the table wobbled. For a moment, everyone stopped breathing. They watched to see if the table would collapse and send the glass crashing.

Another man rushed over and grabbed the table with Señor Gómez. They held it still. The rattling stopped. Everyone breathed again.

Señor Gómez shouted at them. "Get away! You Americans are all alike. You are thiefs. You steal the dolphin and now you try to break my table and my glass treasures."

Mrs. Dawson tugged on Mr. Dawson's arm. Mrs. Bennett pulled Izzy away.

"Wait! My bag—" Izzy stepped back and picked up her bag off the ground. Her eyes met Patti's. "I didn't take it, Patti. Honest."

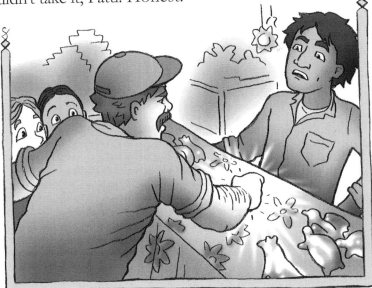

Patti glanced at Señor Gómez and then back at Izzy. "But your uncle—"

Izzy nodded. "I know. He just made everything worse."

Chapter 4

Dolphin Magic

The fun was gone. Totally gone.

Izzy tried not to cry. She said goodbye to Patti
at the hotel. It looked like Patti was trying not to
cry, too. Izzy carefully stepped into the water taxi.
They headed out to the lagoon and Dream Catcher,
the Bennett's boat.

Mrs. Bennett and Mrs. Dawson said nothing.
But Mr. Dawson couldn't stop muttering to his
wife. Izzy couldn't hear much over the boat engine.

She heard enough, though, to know he was mad at Señor Gómez, mad at Patti, and mad at every Mexican.

When the water taxi arrived at Dream Catcher, they all climbed out of the taxi and onto the sailboat. Now even Mr. Dawson had stopped talking.

Izzy headed down the three steps into the boat. She wanted to go to her stateroom and shut the door. But she couldn't. That's where her aunt and uncle were staying.

She turned to go in her mom and dad's stateroom instead. But her mom had already dragged her dad in there. They'd shut the door and were now whispering loudly to each other. At least her dad was whispering loudly. Her mom just kept saying, "Shush. Lower your voice."

Everyone was mad.

Izzy had nowhere to go unless she climbed up into the cockpit again. But her uncle and aunt were up there whispering loudly to each other.

That was the trouble with living on a boat. In that moment, she wished more than anything that she had a backyard. Or a front porch. Or a bike she could hop on and fly away down the street.

Izzy finally decided it didn't matter if her uncle and aunt were staying in her stateroom. She opened the door, crawled up on her berth, and lifted herself out the hatch onto the deck of the boat. She stepped lightly to the bow, or front, of the boat and plopped down. It was as close as she could get to having a backyard.

Katie Kitty found her a few minutes later. The cat slipped into her arms and rubbed its head against her chin. That only made the tears come. Izzy couldn't help it.

Everything was ruined now. Patti would never want to play with her again.

She hated being an only child.

She hated living on a boat.

She hated being away from all of her Seattle friends.

She hated that her uncle had made the mess even more of a mess.

She hated that she'd seen the dolphin, the dolphin from her dreams. And now she'd never have it.

If only her uncle hadn't shouted at Señor Gómez.

If only her uncle hadn't pounded the table.
If only.

Grey clouds swirled in the sky overhead. The wind blew through the lagoon. Behind her, Izzy heard the halyards clang against the mast.

Izzy would never know what magic the dolphin had.

"Izzy," her mom called to her from the cockpit. "Do you want a fresh limeade?"

Izzy sighed. She didn't turn around, but she shook her head no.

She heard footsteps behind her and a thump as her uncle plopped down beside her.

"Hey, kiddo, I'm sorry about all that back at the market."

Izzy didn't turn around.

"It's just that when he called you a thief, it made me so mad. You're my favorite niece—"

"I'm your ONLY niece, Uncle Rob," Izzy said. She groaned a tiny bit at their special joke. "That makes me your LEAST favorite niece, too."

"Izzy, look at me."

She sighed again, but she turned around and looked at him.

"I could have a hundred nieces and you'd still be my favorite. You're a great kid. I know you'd never steal something. It made me really mad when he said that."

"Well, maybe you shouldn't have pounded the table, Uncle Rob," Izzy said.

Mr. Dawson crinkled up his face. "I know. I just should have counted to ten or something before I shouted at him." He tilted his head to one side and shrugged his shoulder. "And you're right. I shouldn't have pounded the table. I'm sorry."

"Thanks, Uncle Rob. I know you were only trying to stick up for me."

"Let's go drink that limeade. All that fresh fruit is at least one thing that's good about Mexico." He squeezed her shoulder. And then he muttered, "Well, it's good as long as we don't get sick."

The five of them sat in the cockpit. Mrs. Bennett served chips and guacamole. They talked about the weather and the Dawson's trip to the boat. They talked about guacamole and learning Spanish. They talked about boating life and where to eat dinner. In fact, they tried to talk about anything except what had happened at the market. But everyone still seemed a little on edge.

Finally, Mrs. Bennett gathered up the glasses and the last few chips. She headed down to the galley to wash the dishes. The others came down to freshen up.

"Izzy, don't forget to put your bag away before we go to dinner," Mrs. Bennett said.

Izzy put her bag on the table. It thunked. She

looked at her mom.

"What do you have in there?" Mrs. Bennett asked. "I thought you didn't buy anything."

Izzy shook her head. "I didn't. It's just my swimsuit and sunscreen." She turned the bag over and dumped the contents.

Out came her sunscreen. Out came her swimsuit.

And then out rolled the most beautiful glass dolphin. Even without the sun shining on it, it sparkled in the late afternoon light.

Chapter 5

Patti? No!

Izzy gasped. "I didn't take the dolphin."

Mrs. Bennett gave her a funny look.

"Honest! I don't know how it got in there."
Izzy took in a sharp breath. She had wanted this
dolphin more than anything. Now that she actually
had it, she felt sick.

But what if the dolphin really was magic?
Could it be?

Mr. Dawson snorted. He put his hands on his

hips. "Well, now we can figure out who stole the dolphin."

"But I—" Izzy shook her head.

"It's what I suspected all along," Mr. Dawson said. "That little friend of yours. What's her name? Patti? She wanted to buy your friendship. So she stole it for you."

"No! I don't believe that," Izzy said. But even as she said it, she wondered. She thought about how Patti had paused when Señor Gómez accused Izzy of stealing. What had been that sound in her voice? The look on her face? Would Patti have stolen the dolphin for her? Izzy had only known Patti for a few weeks. Maybe she really didn't know her at all. Could Patti have done it? It seemed impossible.

But if Patti didn't do it, how did the dolphin get in her bag?

It had to be magic. It just had to be.

Or it had to be Patti.

Izzy's tummy hurt. How could her friend do this to her?

"I tell you, Izzy," Mr. Dawson said. He shook his head. "You just can't trust anyone."

Izzy saw her dad clench his teeth. He looked at Izzy's mom.

"I don't know how the dolphin got in your bag, but it doesn't matter at this point," Mrs. Bennett said. "You just have to return it."

"But if I return it, Señor Gómez will think I took it," Izzy said. Her face felt hot and her eyes watery.

"It doesn't matter what he thinks, Izzy Lizzie. You didn't pay for it, but you have it," Mr. Bennett said. "We'll take it back tomorrow."

"But maybe—" How could she tell her mom and dad about the magic? Adults *never* believed that sort of thing. Even when it was right in front of them.

Patti? No!

Mrs. Bennett scrunched up her nose. "The *tianguis* are here only on Thursdays. The sellers go to a different town every day. We can't take it back to him until next week."

"Well, then, we'll take it back next week," Mr. Bennett said.

"No!" Izzy said.

Everyone looked at her. Mr. Bennett raised an eyebrow.

"I mean, I can't feel like this for a whole week."

Mrs. Bennett hugged Izzy. "Sweetheart, I don't think we have any choice."

Izzy held her breath. She didn't want to cry again. "Maybe the market is still open," she said.

"Maybe," Mrs. Bennett said. "If we hurry, Señor Gómez might still be in the plaza."

They had a plan. It wasn't a great plan as far as Izzy was concerned. But it was a plan. If Izzy could choose, the dolphin would just disappear like it did before, but it wouldn't appear again in her bag.

Wouldn't that be magic, too?

The five of them climbed into Ringee Dingee and headed for shore. They pulled up to the dinghy dock at Hotel Siesta just as Señora Cruz came out of the restaurant. *"¡Hola! Buenas tardes,"* she said. Hello. Good afternoon.

It seemed to Izzy that Señora Cruz wasn't as friendly as usual. But maybe that was just her imagination.

"Hola, Señora Cruz," Mrs. Bennett said. "Did you hear about this afternoon?"

Señora Cruz looked at Izzy and then looked at Mr. Dawson. *"Sí. I have heard."*

Izzy felt miserable. She wanted this settled. *"¿Señora Cruz, está Patti aquí?"* Is Patti here?

"Sí. Un momento." Yes, just a minute. She turned and disappeared up the steps to the rooms where the family lived. A few minutes later, she returned.

Patti trailed a half step behind her.

"Hola, Patti."

"Hola."

Now Izzy was stuck. Patti looked as unhappy as Izzy felt. Izzy didn't know what to say. At all.

"Patti, I don't know how to tell you this." Izzy paused. She looked at her mom and dad. They both nodded. Mrs. Bennett squeezed Izzy's hand. It gave Izzy a tiny bit of courage.

She took a deep breath.

"Patti, when I emptied my bag this afternoon, I found the dolphin. It was in my bag."

Patti tilted her head to one side. "What?"

"I found the dolphin in my bag. I don't know how it got there. But I didn't put it there." Izzy hoped, hoped, hoped that Patti wouldn't say she'd put it there. If Patti hadn't put it there, it really would be magic.

Patti looked very confused. "You found it? In

your bag? How did it get there?"

Izzy wanted to feel relieved. Could she trust that Patti really didn't know either?

"I don't know—"

"Oh, don't give us that look," Mr. Dawson said.

Izzy closed her eyes. She wanted her uncle to stop talking.

"Izzy didn't take the dolphin, so that meant you did it," Mr. Dawson said.

"What?" Patti's eyebrows flew up.

Izzy shook her head and looked at Patti.

"Admit it," Mr. Dawson said. "I don't know why you did it."

"Rob—" Mrs. Dawson started to talk.

Mr. Dawson gave his wife a look that said stop talking. He turned to the Bennetts. "Don't you know by now you can't trust anyone?"

Mrs. Bennett squeezed Izzy's hand again. She said, "Patti, we don't think you took the dolphin.

We don't know how it got in Izzy's bag. But we want to take it back to Señor Gómez."

Tears brimmed Patti's eyes. "I didn't take the dolphin. I don't know how it got in Izzy's bag."

She turned to her mother and said something in Spanish. Señora Cruz glared at Mr. Dawson. No one could mistake what she thought.

"My daughter is not a thief." She spit out every word and crossed her arms. "I will take the girls to the *tianguis*. We will go to Señor Gómez and

explain it all to him." And then she said again, "My daughter is not a thief."

More than anything, Izzy wanted Señora Cruz to add, "And Izzy isn't a thief either."

But she didn't.

Izzy's held her breath so she wouldn't start crying.

Chapter 6

The First Wish

Señora Cruz marched the girls out of the restaurant, through the hotel, and onto the street. She walked fast. The girls had to trot to keep up with her. Izzy worried she'd trip on the cobblestones.

They passed one of the many small grocery stores, or *abarrotes*. A toothless old man sat out front beside the crates of pineapples and bananas. He called to Señora Cruz and waved her over with his hat. She glanced back at the girls and then stopped for a moment to chat.

The girls stood in the street and waited. Izzy's tummy felt all jumpy. "What are we going to say to Señor Gómez ?" she whispered to Patti.

"I don't know. The truth, I guess."

The truth.

Did the truth include the dream about the dolphin?

And the magic?

"The truth is, I didn't steal it." Izzy looked her friend in the eyes. "Do you believe me, Patti?"

Patti nodded her head slowly. "I believe you." She glanced over at her mom and then at Izzy again. "I didn't steal it either. Do you believe me?"

Izzy looked at her friend. She listened to her voice. She watched her face. Either Patti was telling the truth or she could be in the movies with her acting skills. Izzy nodded her head. "I believe you."

The First Wish

Patti's face relaxed a tiny bit. "Good. I was afraid you believed your uncle."

Izzy shook her head. "I didn't want to believe him. But sometimes a little seed gets planted in your brain. Know what I mean?"

"That sounds funny." Patti giggled and scrunched up her nose. "I don't know what that means exactly. But I think I understand. The seed is like an idea?"

Izzy nodded. "And once it's there, it just grows bigger and bigger."

"Well, I think THAT idea was more like a weed."

The girls laughed. Izzy felt a tiny bit better. Maybe if she told Patti about the dream, it would all make more sense.

Señora Cruz looked over her shoulder at the girls. But she turned back and kept talking with the old man.

Izzy just wanted this misery over.

The girls sighed and sat down on the curb. And then Patti said what they both were thinking, "But we still don't know what we're going to say. We don't know how the dolphin got in your bag."

Izzy's stomach starting feeling jumpy again. She knew only one way to explain how the dolphin got there. It sounded so nuts. She hated to even say it. She peeked over Patti's head at Señora Cruz, who still rattled away in Spanish with the old man.

"This is going to sound crazy, Patti." It was now or never. She had to trust her friend. "I have an idea how the dolphin got in my bag."

Patti raised her eyebrows. "How?"

Izzy looked around again. No one could hear her, she was sure. "Remember how Señor Gómez said it was magic?"

"*¿Magia?*" Patti said. Her eyes grew wide.

Izzy nodded. "I didn't take it and you didn't

take it. I think it really is magic. That's how it ended up in my bag."

"Is it possible?" Patti asked.

"How else do you explain it?" Izzy's heart thumped in her chest. "Here's the other thing." She looked at Señora Cruz and the toothless old man. She scanned the street.

Izzy hoped her friend didn't think she was crazy. "This morning I had a dream about the dolphin."

Patti looked puzzled. "A dream? *Un sueño?*"

Izzy nodded. "In the dream there was a real dolphin like the glass dolphin. It sparkled. It had these strange blue lines along its back."

A gust of wind swirled the dust in the street and blew the curtains in a window across the street. Above them, dark clouds gathered in the sky.

"Just like this dolphin," Patti said. She looked very serious.

Izzy nodded again.

Patti whispered something in Spanish. And then she whispered it in English. "It has to be magic. There's no other way to explain it. But what kind of magic do you think it is?"

"Maybe it's like Aladdin's lamp. Do you know that story?"

"Aladdin? Of course." Patti laughed. "Everyone knows that story. I even have the DVD."

"Then you know Aladdin just rubbed the lamp and got three wishes."

"But that man came out of the lamp. I don't know the word in English."

"The genie?" Izzy said. "True. There's no way a genie will come out if we rub the dolphin. But we could still make a wish."

She opened her bag and took out the glass treasure. It sparkled in the late afternoon sun. The light shone through it, scattering colors onto the street.

"It's more beautiful than ever," Patti said.

"Maybe we'll get three wishes. What do we have to lose?" Izzy asked. "I say we both hold the dolphin. I make the wish in English and—"

"And I make the wish in Spanish," Patti finished.

The girls both held half the dolphin. Izzy held the nose and Patti the tail. They closed their eyes.

"I wish everything gets fixed and I can keep the dolphin," Izzy said. She rubbed the smooth glass.

Patti repeated the wish in Spanish.

The girls opened their eyes and looked at each other.

The wind clattered the leaves in the palm tree beside them. Thunder rumbled once overhead and then again off in the distance.

"Do you think it worked?" Patti asked.

"I don't know. Did you feel something? Like a buzz or a tingle?"

Patti's eyes shifted to the side and then back to Izzy. "I don't know. Did you?"

Izzy's eyes shifted, too. "Well, I'm not sure. Maybe."

"Do you think it worked?" Patti asked again.

Señora Cruz called to them, *"Vengan niñas."* Come, girls.

"We'll soon find out," Izzy said.

The First Wish

They got up and brushed the dirt from their shorts. The three of them started their march again to *el jardín*.

Two blocks later they entered the plaza. Most of the vendors still had their things out for sale. A few of them had already packed away their goods.

Izzy's heart began to pound again. She wanted to believe in the magic of the dolphin.

They passed the wooden bowl stand. They passed the stand with the berries and the one with the *piñatas*. They passed the old woman with the *molé* and the straw hat stand. Finally, they reached Señor Gómez's stand.

He was gone.

Patti looked at Izzy. "He's not here. That means you can't return the dolphin."

Izzy felt lightheaded. She whispered to her friend, "The magic worked!"

Thunder boomed.

Chapter 7

The Second Wish

Señora Cruz was not happy. The whole way back to the restaurant, she chattered away in Spanish to Patti. So Patti wasn't happy either.

Mr. and Mrs. Bennett and the Dawsons sat at a table in the restaurant. An empty basket of chip crumbs sat in front of them. They didn't look all that happy either.

"Señor Gómez is gone. They said he left early." Señora Cruz looked at Mr. Dawson. "He did not have a good day."

Izzy's stomach was all jumpy again.

Señora Cruz continued, "We know where Señor Gómez lives. Most nights he is not home until 8:00 or 9:00. But since he left already, he will be home early. Izzy will take the dolphin back. She will tell him what happened."

Izzy's heart pounded. It was the worst plan she could think of. She wished she could whisper to her mom about the magic of the dolphin. If her mom believed her, maybe she could keep the dolphin forever.

"Patti will go with Izzy," Señora Cruz continued.

For one second, Izzy felt a tiny bit better.

Then Señora Cruz pointed at Mr. Dawson. "And you will go, too."

"What?" Izzy whispered under her breath. She couldn't believe what Señora Cruz had just said.

It didn't matter though.

Minutes later, Patti and Izzy once again marched out of the restaurant, through the hotel, and onto the street. This time, Mr. Dawson followed a few feet behind them.

Lightening flashed. Seconds later, thunder boomed. A few fat drops of rain splattered on the street, making little dust puddles where they landed.

The three of them walked faster.

"What was your mother thinking?" Izzy whispered to Patti. She glanced back at her uncle. Izzy didn't even want to think about what he might say to Señor Gómez. It seemed like the worst possible thing to do.

"I think she wasn't thinking," Patti whispered back. She looked just as scared as Izzy felt. "Why does your uncle say those mean things?"

"I don't know. He's fun most of the time."

Izzy turned to look at her uncle again. He kept glancing around like he thought someone was going to jump out at him.

It made her nervous.

"What if he says something awful to Señor Gómez again?" Patti asked.

Izzy shook her head. "We'll just have to hope Señor Gómez doesn't say something mean back."

A gust of wind swirled the dust in the street ahead of them. Above them, the gaps in the dark clouds grew. Izzy could see patches of blue. Maybe the storm would miss them.

The three of them stopped as a battered old city bus came around the corner. To Izzy, it looked like someone had taken a school bus, repainted it white and blue, and then drove it for a million miles. The front windshield had an ugly crack in it, like a rock had hit it. Dents and scrapes covered the sides.

"This is our bus," Patti said.

Izzy looked at her uncle. His eyes scanned the beat up vehicle. He didn't look happy, but he climbed onto the bus with them.

The girls took a seat together. Mr. Dawson stood next to them in the aisle even though the bus had plenty of empty benches farther back.

"It's okay, Uncle Rob," Izzy said. "You can sit down back there." She motioned with her head. "We'll be safe."

Mr. Dawson looked the passengers over. He paused a few seconds. When the bus jolted forward, he lost his balance and then caught it again. That seemed to convince him to sit down. Izzy heard him grumbling quietly. She couldn't make out the words, but she hoped no one understood English near where he sat.

The bus rumbled through town. They passed the plaza, *el jardín*. Now most of the owners of the stalls, or *puestos,* had packed up for the day.

"How far away does Señor Gómez live?" Izzy asked.

The Second Wish

Patti shrugged her shoulders. "Not so far."

To the west, the sun peeked through the storm clouds and slowly settled into the sea. Colors exploded in the sky. Reds, yellows, oranges, and pinks. Izzy wished she had crayons and paper to make a picture of it. Sometimes sunsets were the best part of the day. She wanted to remember this one.

Even though it was growing darker, the town seemed to come more alive. They passed houses that had turned into tiny restaurants with two or three tables out front. Onions and peppers sizzled next to roasting chickens or grilling beef. The smell drove Izzy crazy. Every place they passed had a grandmother patting out fresh tortillas. Izzy's stomach growled. She remembered she hadn't eaten anything except some chips and guacamole since lunch. That was before the dolphin disappeared and then showed up again in her bag.

That was before her life turned upside down.

How good could the magic be if things were still such a mess?

They whizzed by a stand of fresh coconuts chopped open. Each one had a straw stuck inside. Izzy wished she could stop and sip some coconut milk.

Children played in the street. They laughed and shrieked as they ran. On one corner, a small group of kids filled a bucket with water balloons. Izzy wanted to stop and join their little army. She would gladly get soaked in a water fight rather than go to Señor Gómez's house.

Izzy twisted back and looked at her uncle. He looked worried. She wondered what he thought of the bus ride. Did he see the dusty floor and broken windows? The trash in the aisle and the chipped paint on the seats?

Or did he see the happy teenage couple flirting with each other? She hoped he saw the tired young mother and her sweet baby with the shy smile and sleepy chocolate-colored eyes. She hoped, too, he noticed the worn out people riding the bus home from work. Izzy knew Mexico wasn't as clean and tidy as the US. But her mom always said to look past that. When Izzy did, she always saw people who reminded her of people in Seattle. They had families and jobs and worries and things that made them sad and happy just like the people she knew at home.

She hoped her uncle could see that too.

It grew darker as they left the center of town. Fewer corners had streetlights.

"How much farther?" Izzy asked.

"I'm not sure. But I'll know the street where we get off," Patti said. She lowered her voice and asked, "What do you think your uncle is thinking right now?"

"I think he's worried we're going to get kidnapped and dragged out into the jungle and robbed."

Patti laughed. "In Barra?"

It made Izzy feel a tiny bit better even though she worried just a little about that, too. Her tummy felt upside down about so many things.

Don't worry? Be happy?

Not a chance, Izzy thought. That dolphin had it totally wrong.

"I think we need to make another wish," Patti said.

The Second Wish

"About the dolphin?" Izzy asked.

Patti shook her head. "About your uncle."

Izzy looked back. Her uncle's fingers clenched the seatback in front of him. He seemed ready to jump out of the bus.

"He really is a nice man, Patti. He comes to all my school plays. He never forgets my birthday. He laughs at my jokes. He's lots of fun when he's not nervous. He's just not good in new situations. You have to believe me." Izzy sighed.

"That's why we have to make a wish," Patti said. She poked Izzy with her elbow.

Izzy nodded. She pulled the smooth, glass dolphin out of her bag. Each girl held half the dolphin. This time, though, Patti held the head and Izzy held the tail.

Patti began, "We're going to wish your uncle learns to like Mexicans."

"No," Izzy said. "It's not about Mexicans. It's

about anything that's new for him. We're going to wish that he treats everyone the same, even if they're not just like him. We'll wish that he's not so suspicious." That word her dad had used now made total sense.

"Suspicious? I don't know this word," Patti said.

"It means that he doesn't trust people at first."

"Yes, that's what we wish for. That he starts to trust people, even if he doesn't know them," Patti said.

The girls held the dolphin. They closed their eyes. Patti made her wish first in Spanish. Izzy followed in English.

Izzy opened her eyes and looked back at her uncle. He didn't look any different. Her tummy didn't feel any better, but she had a little hope in her heart.

The magic worked once. It had to work again.

It just had to.

Chapter 8

Facing Señor Gómez

Patti stood up. "This is our stop."

The three of them hopped down from the bus.

They turned a corner and found themselves on a dirt street. A white dog with black spots trotted out to meet them. It stopped in front of them and sniffed their sandals as they passed. The dog growled and Izzy worried it might bite them. But it soon lost interest in the girls. It wandered off to a bag of trash and started sniffing something else.

The cheery lights of the town seemed far away now, even though they'd walked only a block or two from the bus stop. Trees lined the street. They swayed in a slight breeze. All around them Izzy could only see shadows.

"So is this a dangerous neighborhood, Patti?" Izzy asked. She realized this was the second time that day she'd asked her friend this kind of question.

"Huh?"

"Are we safe walking here at night?"

Patti waited a second too long to answer. But she said, "Yes. We're okay." Her voice didn't match her words.

Izzy wished Patti had answered faster or that her voice didn't sound shaky. Izzy twisted back and looked at her uncle. His eyes darted in every direction. His hands were clenched into fists. For the first time that day, Izzy was glad to have him so close.

People stood in doorways. Izzy could see their outlines. She wondered if they were watching them.

She wondered, too, if Patti and she should be walking faster. Or maybe they should run. The bag with the glass dolphin felt heavy on her shoulder.

"How much farther?" Izzy asked. Her own voice sounded shaky. She wondered if Patti could hear how nervous she felt.

"Not much." Patti's voice quivered a little. Izzy didn't like that.

Ahead of them, the moon rose through the storm clouds. It looked like a giant orange ball on the tops of the trees. It cast a strange but soft light on the street.

They walked without talking. Izzy's heart pounded. She wished she could be back on Dream Catcher with Katie Kitty. She wished she could be all cozy in her berth and reading a book.

She wished she'd never seen the glass dolphin.

No. That wasn't true. She still wanted it more than anything.

Patti stopped suddenly and pointed to a house the color of the sun. "That's it. That's where Señor Gómez lives."

The house stood a few feet from the street. It looked small to Izzy, maybe the size of a garage that would hold only one car. Yellow light drifted from two small windows. A plastic three-wheeled trike, a baseball bat and ball, and a rubber basketball lay scattered on the yard. A short plastic basketball stand and hoop leaned against the house. A beat up old pickup truck sat in the dirt drive. Tubs and a folded table filled the truck bed.

Izzy swallowed. She looked at her friend.

"This it?" Mr. Dawson said.

Patti nodded.

"It's pretty small."

Patti nodded again.

Facing Señor Gómez

"Not much yard."

Izzy shook her head.

"Looks like they've got a kid. Must be a boy."

Izzy nodded her head. She remembered sweet little Pancho.

All three of them took a deep breath.

"Okay. Let's get this over with," Mr. Dawson said.

They marched up to the front door. Patti knocked. They could hear TV noise coming from the room and then no sound.

A short, plump woman in a faded flowered dress opened the door.

"Hola, Señora Gómez," Patti said.

"Hola, buenas noches," the woman said. Hello, good evening.

"¿Está el Señor Gómez?" Is Señor Gómez here?

"Sí." She said something to Patti in Spanish. The woman opened the door and welcomed them in.

"She said Señor Gómez just got home from his day at the *tianguis,"* Patti said. "They are just now eating dinner."

The three of them stepped into the small space of the living room. Only it wasn't really a living room like Izzy knew from Seattle. It was a tiny space with a short couch and a table and three chairs that didn't match each other. The kitchen had three concrete shelves with dishes, pots and pans, and a few cans on them. A worn kitchen sink stood between a narrow stove and short refrigerator. A picture of Jesus on the cross hung next to the stove and another picture of Jesus hung on the wall over the couch.

A curtain hid the back of the room. But through a gap in the fabric, Izzy could see two neatly made beds and a dresser covered with photos.

Señor Gómez and Pancho both sat at the table eating tortillas and what looked like rice and refried beans. Pancho wore pajamas with trucks on them. His black hair lay in a halo of wet spikes like he had just taken a bath. Pancho laughed and jumped down from his chair and ran to the girls. "Izzy, Izzy!" he said. He lifted his arms up to Izzy. She bent down and gave him a quick hug. His breath smelled like tortillas, but his skin smelled sweet like peaches.

Señor Gómez stood up. He seemed confused.

Better that than angry, Izzy thought.

She looked at her uncle, who looked at the room around them. He seemed confused too, even though he shouldn't have been. He knew why they were there.

"*Hola, buenas noches, Señor Gómez,*" Patti said.

Izzy couldn't believe how brave Patti sounded.

"*Hola,*" Señor Gómez said and nodded at them.

Patti looked at Izzy.

Izzy stood up. She felt jittery and her voice shook.

"*Hola, Señor Gómez,*" she began. "I came because . . . " Izzy didn't know what to say next. She really wished she had practiced what to say with Patti. Now it was too late. She started again. "When I got back to the boat, I found this in my bag." She set her bag on the table and pulled out the glass dolphin.

There. It was done. Almost.

"I don't know how it got in my bag." She didn't say anything about the magic. She hoped he would just know. "I want you to know I didn't steal it." Izzy stopped. She waited for Señor Gómez to say something, but he didn't. Izzy looked at Patti. She looked at her uncle. Finally, she said, "I didn't steal it. I hope you believe me."

Señor Gómez took the dolphin from her. He turned it over in his hands several times and ran his fingers over the smooth glass. Then he set it on the table and turned to her. To Izzy, it seemed like forever before he spoke.

"I believe you," he finally said. "I don't think you steal the dolphin and then return it. I don't know how the dolphin is in your bag, but I think you are an honest girl."

All afternoon and evening, Izzy had felt like her chest would explode. And now, she felt so relieved all she could do was laugh.

"¡Gracias! Thank you, Señor Gómez."

Señor Gómez looked at Mr. Dawson. He started to say something but then stopped. He shook his head then said to Izzy. "Because you do this thing, I give you a small gift. Is important to be honest."

He disappeared behind the curtain where the beds were. A moment later, he returned with a shoebox. He dug through it until he found a small silver charm about the size of a penny.

"You like dolphins? I give you a little dolphin. Is not glass, but is still beautiful." Señor Gómez handed Izzy a shiny dolphin. "Is for a bracelet or necklace. Wear it and remember why you get this."

Patti and Izzy looked at each other. "It's a dolphin. And you get to keep it," Patti said under her breath. "The magic worked."

Izzy took the charm. Her eyes felt watery. Her heart pounded a little too. The magic *had* worked. Maybe not like they thought it would, but something had happened.

"Thank you, Señor Gómez. I will wear this forever. And I will always think of today."

Facing Señor Gómez

Mr. Dawson finally found his voice. It sounded hoarse and funny. "This is very kind of you, Mr. Gómez." He paused and took a deep breath. His chest moved up and down. "And I'm sorry for what I said today. I can see you are a hardworking man. You are not a thief."

Señor Gómez smiled slightly and nodded his head. "Gracias, señor. I am sorry, too, that I said what I did." He reached out his hand. Mr. Dawson paused and then reached

his hand out to Señor Gómez. They shook hands like friends should.

Izzy glanced at Patti. Her uncle wasn't suspicious. The second wish had come true. Patti nodded her head. She knew.

Mr. Dawson put his hands on Izzy and Patti's shoulders. "I think it's time we let you finish your supper. And time for these girls to head back to the hotel."

They turned to go.

"Wait a minute," Izzy said. "I almost forgot my bag."

She picked it up and threw it over her shoulder. But it didn't feel right. It felt heavier. Something banged against her back.

"Oh no!" Izzy looked at the empty spot on the table where the dolphin had been. She looked at Señor Gómez. Slowly she reached into her bag and pulled out a beautiful glass dolphin.

A magical glass dolphin.

Facing Señor Gómez

Patti's hands flew to her mouth. "Is it what we think? Is it really magic?"

"What? How can this be?" Izzy paused. It HAD to be magic.

Señor Gómez's eyes grew narrow. "Do you think I am a fool that—"

Mr. Dawson jumped in before he could finish. His voice sounded loud and angry. "Don't even think about accusing Izzy—"

Sweet little Pancho laughed his bubbly laugh.

And suddenly Izzy knew.

"Wait," Izzy said. "Just wait." She looked at the two men. She looked at Patti.

"Maybe it's magic. But probably not," Izzy said. She laughed because she realized who made the dolphin disappear both times. And it wasn't magic.

"Pancho!" She reached her arms out to the little boy. "Did you put the dolphin in my bag today?" Patti repeated Izzy's question in Spanish.

The little boy giggled and flew into Izzy's arms

and hugged her. *"Sí. Tres veces."* He held up two fingers.

"Three times?" Izzy said. "I think you mean two. *Uno, dos."* Izzy counted on his fingers in Spanish. "But why? *¿Por qué?* "

"¡Me gusta el pelo rojo!" He touched her red hair. He rattled off more Spanish.

"He says he loves your red hair," Patti said. "He wants you to be happy. He wants you to have the dolphin."

Izzy kissed Pancho on the top of his head. She stood up and handed the glass dolphin back to Señor Gómez. "Pancho is a very special little boy. But I think you should hold the dolphin till we leave. I don't want to find it in my bag one more time."

Pancho grabbed his dad's leg and hugged it. Señor Gómez picked up his son and kissed him on the cheek. He looked at the girls. And then he shook his head. *"No, Señorita,"* he said. "I want you to keep it. I have learned a very important lesson today about trusting people."

"You want me to keep it?" Izzy could hardly believe what he'd just said.

Mr. Dawson shook his head. He took out his wallet. "You are generous to give the dolphin to Izzy." He handed some pesos to Señor Gómez. "But I can see you are not a rich man. I want to pay for the dolphin." Mr. Dawson turned to Izzy. "I've learned an important lesson today, too. People are people. I shouldn't be suspicious of them just because they're different from me."

Izzy and Patti looked at each other and laughed.

Izzy gave her uncle a big hug. And then she handed the silver dolphin charm to Patti. "This should be yours."

"Why would you give this to me?"

"Because you are the best friend I could ever have. You are so brave. The glass dolphin will remind me of the silver dolphin and you forever." And then she whispered, "Maybe, just maybe, this charm has a little magic too."

Chapter 9

The Third (and Best!) Wish

Mr. Dawson and Señor Gómez shook hands again. Izzy and Patti hugged Pancho one more time. Patti promised to invite him to swim with Izzy and her at the hotel. Then Mr. Dawson, Patti, and Izzy headed back down the street to the bus stop.

"I think we have one more wish," Izzy whispered to Patti as they walked. She liked the weight of the dolphin in her bag. It didn't matter if it had real magic or not.

Patti smiled. "How about a wish for ice cream?

That would be a perfect way to celebrate."

Izzy laughed. "I have a better idea. Let's wish that our friendship lasts forever." She pulled out the dolphin.

"That's the best idea yet," Patti said.

They each held part of the dolphin and wished their wish in English and in Spanish.

"I don't think we needed a third wish," Patti said. "But that's the best way to use it if we had one."

"The very best," Izzy said.

The sun had set completely by now. Only a touch of orange colored the sky to the west. It left the street dark and full of spooky shadows. They could only see crazy patches of light in the cloudless sky where the moonlight shone through the trees. Chickens clucked and a rooster crowed. Just ahead, two dogs barked and ran into the street to see who dared walk past. People sat on their front steps and visited in the cooler evening air. Patti knew a couple of them. She called to them and waved.

Behind them, Izzy heard an engine start up. She turned and saw a car creep out into the middle of the street. The headlights came on. The driver flashed the headlights at them.

The three of them moved to the side of the street, but the car didn't move any faster. The driver flashed the headlights again.

Izzy glanced back at the car. She could see four people in the car. All adults. It made her nervous that they moved so slowly.

"You're sure this is a safe place to walk at night, Patti?" Izzy asked.

She paused but said, "Yes."

Izzy didn't like how Patti's voice shook a little. Izzy was determined to be brave, though.

Mr. Dawson said, "We'll be fine." He took the

girls' hands and headed toward the bus stop. Izzy noticed they moved a little faster.

The car drew nearly even with them now. The driver honked the horn.

"Patti, Izzy," a voice called from the car.

"*¿Mamá?*" Patti laughed.

"Mom? Dad? Aunt Ella—" Izzy said.

"Get in," Señora Cruz stopped the car. "We came to get you, but we didn't see you come out of Señor Gómez's house. It's a good thing you know people in the neighborhood, Patti. We heard your voice."

Mr. Dawson, Patti, and Izzy squeezed into the back seat with Mrs. Bennett and Mrs. Dawson.

"How did it go?" They all asked at once.

"Better than you could ever have guessed," Mr. Dawson said. He reached over and tousled Izzy's hair. "We have a couple of brave, smart girls here."

Izzy could see Señora Cruz in the rearview

mirror. Señora Cruz smiled and winked at Izzy.

"Hey, I'm starving," Mr. Dawson said. "Any chance you can make more of those great enchiladas you served at lunch? I hear they're pretty amazing." He paused and added, "And then I'm buying everyone ice cream."

Izzy and Patti just looked at each other and laughed.

No worries. Izzy was happy.

Sneak peek of the next book

Mystery of the Naga at Night

Chapter One

Jess' right eyelid opened a teeny tiny crack. She heard it again. A rustling noise. Where was it coming from? No matter. Probably just part of her dream. She rolled over to her side and snuggled up in her blanket. Her right eyelid, heavy and ready to snooze, slowly started to shut.

Closer now. The rustling. Jess just wanted to sleep. She hated this dream. Why couldn't she dream of unicorns and rainbows instead of scary rustling sounds?

Jess turned back over and sighed. And then she heard the sounds once more. Louder now. Rustling. And crunching. Both of her eyes popped open. Definitely NOT a dream. Something was creeping closer and closer to her window. What could be out there?

At home in Boston, she'd hear brakes squealing or the whap of cars driving over a manhole cover. But this didn't sound like Boston traffic. Still groggy, she rubbed her eyes and shook her head. The shapes in the room confused her. Where was her dresser? And lamp? Why did it smell so different? Like a market in the jungle. With lemons . . . no, oranges. And grass. And mint. And fish? Where was she anyway?

She blinked her eyes and sat up in bed. Now she started to remember. Chiang Mai, Thailand. Last night they traveled in the back of a bouncy old pickup truck to a hill tribe village outside of Chiang Mai. She was here with her mom to help with the village school.

Rustle. Crunch. Rustle. Crunch.

Jess froze. What could be outside her window

here in Chiang Mai? She had absolutely NO idea. And having no idea made the noises even scarier. Whatever it was sounded close enough to touch. Jess' heart pounded.

She slowly rolled her feet over to the cool cement floor and stood up. Her knees shook underneath her. She crooked her neck and peered out the open window in her room.

The wind blew. Pebbles crunched. A shadow moved.

Acckkk! Her knees fell out from under her. She stumbled away from the window just as the shadow moved closer.

Jess clamped her eyes shut and ducked back into her bed. Her heart pounded so fast it felt ready to burst out of her chest.

The noise continued. Rustle. Crunch. Rustle. Crunch. Willing herself to be brave, she peered out the window once more. Her sleepy eyes strained to find the moving shadow again.

She really wished she would just see a unicorn or a rainbow. Except that a unicorn might actually be scary too, especially if since she'd never seen one before. Sleepy as she was, Jess knew she wouldn't see rainbows in the dark.

What she saw was certainly no unicorn. Or rainbow . . .

Find out what happens to Jess and Nong May in the next Pack-n-Go Girls book, Mystery of the Naga at Night.

Dive into More Reading Fun with Izzy and Patti!

Coming Soon!

Mystery of the Not So Empty Room

Patti invites Izzy to a quinceañera party
and Izzy is beyond excited! As they get
closer to the special day, though, things
start to fall apart. First, Patti's brother,
Carlos, disappears. And then a room that's
supposed to be empty is anything but.

Coming Soon!

Mystery of the Missing Key

Patti is thrilled to finally visit her friend
Izzy in Seattle. Izzy is eager to show
Patti around the city. But that has to
wait since Izzy has a funeral to go to.
It's the very last thing the girls expect to
do on their very first day together again.
As they leave the graveside, a strange

man approaches Izzy and shoves an ancient wooden box
into her hands. "For you," he says and disappears. Inside the
box is a single piece of paper with three words: Find the key.

Meet More Pack-n-Go Girls!

Discover Austria with Brooke and Eva!

Mystery of the Ballerina Ghost

Nine-year-old Brooke Mason is headed to Austria. She'll stay in Schloss Mueller, and ancient Austrian castle. Eva, the girl who lives in Schloss Mueller, is thrilled to meet Brooke. Unfortunately, the castle's ghost isn't quite so happy.

Don't miss the second Austria book, *Mystery of the Secret Room.*

Discover Thailand with Jess and Nong May!

Mystery of the Golden Temple

Nong May and her family have had a lot of bad luck lately. When nine-year-old Jess arrives in Thailand and accidentally breaks a special family treasure, it seems to only get worse. It turns out the treasure holds a secret that could change things forever! Coming soon: *Mystery of the Naga at Night.*

What to Know Before You Go!

How Big Is Mexico?

Mexico is the fifteenth largest country in the world. It's the same size as the state of Alaska, which tells you how huge Alaska is! The United States is about five times as big as Mexico. But we only have about three times as many people. Mexico has more Spanish speaking people than any other country in the world.

Mexican Money

Did you know that every country has its own money? In the United States, we use dollars and cents for our money system. Mexicans use pesos and centavos.

We use this symbol to mean dollar: $. The symbol for the peso is the same: $. So if you go shopping in Mexico, don't be confused. They only list prices in pesos.

If you go to Mexico, you won't be able to use American dollars or your quarters, dimes, or nickels. Instead, your mom and dad can go to a bank to change their dollars for pesos. Or they can use an ATM to get money from their bank account. The money that comes out of the bank machine will be pesos, of course!

Places to Explore

When most people plan a trip to Mexico, they only think about going to the beach because Mexico is so well known for its beaches. It has thousands of miles of Pacific and Caribbean coastline. But some of the best places to visit in Mexico aren't near the water. The country has fascinating ruins that date back thousands of years. Did you know that Mexico City has pyramids like Egypt? Mexico also has jungles and remote mountain areas. Most places away from the beach are cheap, even if they aren't always the easiest to get to.

What Mexicans Eat

You can find Mexican food almost anywhere in the United States. So you probably already have favorite Mexican dishes. Tacos, burritos, and enchiladas are the most common. Make sure you also try fajitas, guacamole, and flan. Mexican food is often spicier than American food, but it's also full of flavor.

Recipe for Enchiladas de Patti

Be sure to get an adult to help you with the chopping and sautéing.

Chop, sauté, and mix the following together:
- 1 chopped onion
- 1 clove garlic, finely chopped
- 8 oz. fresh mushrooms, sliced
- 1 jalapeno pepper, seeded and finely chopped [Be sure to wash your hands after touching the pepper!]
- 2 teaspoons cumin
- 1 teaspoon pepper
- 1/2 teaspoon salt

Add:
- 8 oz. sour cream
- 7 oz. salsa verde [find this in the Mexican food section]
- 1/4 cup chopped cilantro
- 2 cups shredded Monterey Jack cheese
- 2 cups cooked and shredded chicken

Put 1/2 cup of the mixture into an 8" flour tortilla and roll it up. You'll need 10-12 tortillas. Put the rolled up tortillas into a 9" x 13" pan. It's okay to pack them in tightly.

Mix and pour over the enchiladas:
- 8 oz. sour cream
- 7 oz. salsa verde

Bake at 325 degrees for 35 minutes. During the last 10 minutes of baking, spread 2 cups of shredded Monterey Jack cheese over the top.

Say It in Spanish!

English	Spanish	Spanish Pronunciation
Hello	Hola	OH-la
Good day	Buenos días	BWEH-nohs DEE-ahs
Good afternoon	Buenos tardes	BWEH-nohs TAR-dehs
Good evening/good night	Buenos noches	BWEH-nohs NOH-cheh
Goodbye	Adiós	Ah-DEE-OHS
See you later	Hasta luego	Ah-sta loo-A-go
Please	Por favor	Poor fah-VOR
Thank you	Gracias	GRAH-see-ahs
Excuse me	Perdone	Pehr-DOHN-eh
You're welcome	De nada	DAY NAH-dah
I'm sorry	Lo siento	Low see-EN-toh
Yes/No	Sí/No	SEE/ NOH
Of course	Por supuesto	Por soo-PWES-toh
How are you?	¿Como estas?	KOH-mo es-TAHS?
Just a moment	Sólo un momento	SO-lo Oon mo-MEN-toh
Market stands	Puestos	PWES-toes
Grocery store	Abarrotes	Ah-bah-ROE-tes
Excuse me	Con permiso	Cone per-ME-so
What a pity	Qué lastima	Kay LAS-tee-mah

114

English	Spanish	Spanish Pronunciation
The plaza	El jardín	Ell har-DEEN
Dangerous	Peligroso	Pel-ih-gro-so
Delicious	Delicioso	Dee-lih-cee-o-so
Dolphin	Delfín	Del-FEEN
Magic	Magia	Mah-HEE-ah
Market	Tianguis	Tee-AHN-geese
Here	Aquí	Ah-KEE
Boy/Girl	Niño/Niña	Neen-yo/Neen-yah
0	Cero	SEH-roh
1	Uno	Oo-noh
2	Dos	Dohs
3	Tres	Trehs
4	Cuatro	KWAH-troh
5	Cinco	SEEN-koh
6	Seis	SEH-ees
7	Siete	Dee-EH-the
8	Ocho	OH-choh
9	Nueve	Noo-EH-beh
10	Diez	Dee-EHS

My Mexican Trip Planner

Where to go: _____

_____

_____

_____

_____

_____

_____

_____

_____

_____

_____

_____

_____

_____

What to do: _____

_____

_____

_____

_____

_____

_____

_____

_____

_____

_____

_____

_____

_____

_____

My Mexican Trip Planner

Things I want to pack:

_____

_____

_____

_____

_____

_____

_____

_____

_____

_____

_____

_____

Friends to send postcards to:

_____

_____

_____

_____

_____

_____

_____

_____

_____

_____

_____

_____

_____

Thank you to the following Pack-n-Go Girls:

Maia Caprice
Abby Rice
Sarah Travis

Thank you also to Linda Bello-Ruiz, Cari Caprice, Marjorie Ehrhardt, Susan Grover, Eli Rainhart, Ashley Rice and Jeannie Sheeks.

And a special thanks to my Pack-n-Go Girls co-founder, Lisa Travis, and our husbands, Steve Diller and Rich Travis, who have been along with us on this adventure.

Janelle Diller has always had a passion for writing. As a young child, she wouldn't leave home without a pad and pencil just in case her novel hit her and she had to scribble it down quickly. She eventually learned that good writing takes a lot more time and effort than this. Fortunately, though, she still loves to write. She's especially lucky because she also loves to travel. It doesn't get any better than writing stories about traveling! Janelle and her husband live on a sailboat in Mexico in the winter and in a house in Colorado in the summer.

Adam Turner has been working as a freelance illustrator since 1987. He has illustrated coloring books, puzzle books, magazine articles, game packaging, and children's books. He's loved to draw ever since he picked up his first pencil as a toddler. Instead of doing the usual two-year-old thing of chewing on it or poking his eye out

with it, he actually put it on paper and thus began the journey. Adam also loves to travel and has had some crazy adventures. He's swum with crocodiles in the Zambizi, jumped out of a perfectly good airplane, and even fished for piranha in the Amazon. It's a good thing drawing relaxes his nerves! Adam lives in St. Paul, Minnesota, with his wife and their daughter.

Pack-n-Go Girls Online

Dying to know when the next Pack-n-Go Girls book will be out? Want to learn more Spanish? Trying to figure out what to pack for your next trip? Looking for cool family travel tips? And teachers, interested in some complimentary learning resources to use while your students are reading *Mystery of the Disappearing Dolphin*?

- Check out our website:
  www.packngogirls.com
- Follow us on Twitter:
  @packngogirls
- Like us on Facebook:
  facebook.com/packngogirls